SLUGS

by
David Greenberg

Illustrated by
Victoria Chess

Little, Brown and Company
BOSTON   NEW YORK   LONDON

To my Mother, Father, Family, and she to whom I refer

D. G.

For Sam William Dickerson

V. C.

Library of Congress Cataloging in Publication Data

Greenberg, David (David T.)
  Slugs.

  Summary: Suggests many unpleasant things that can be done with and to slugs and warns that even the lowly slug may have its revenge.
  [1. Snails — Fiction. 2. Stories in rhyme]
I. Chess, Victoria, ill. II. Title.
PZ8.3.G755S   1983   [E]   82-10017
ISBN 0-316-32658-5 (hc)   AACR2
ISBN 0-316-32659-3 (pb)

HC: 15 14 13
PB: 20 19 18

PRINTED IN THE UNITED STATES OF AMERICA

WOR

Swallow a Slug
By its tail or its snout
Feel it slide down
Feel it climb out

3

Nibble on its feetsies
Nibble on its giblets
Nibble on its bellybutton
Nibble on its riblets

Breakfast? Slug juice
Slug soup's great for lunch
Fry 'em like potatoes
Love the way they crunch

5

Tie one on a leash
Take it for a walk
Take your Slug to school today
Teach it how to talk

Hang them from a Christmas tree
Mix them with your Easter sweets
Carve one like a pumpkin
Hand them out for trick-or-treats

7

Perch one on a doorknob
Or on a toilet seat
Sizzle them on light bulbs
Squash them with your feet

Dissect a Slug with scissors
Poke one with a tweezer
Pop one in the microwave
Freeze one in the freezer

9

Take a Slug
Squeeze its liver
Watch it wiggle
Feel it quiver

10

Stuff one in an envelope
Mail it to a friend
Drop one in the blender
Turn it on to blend

11

Try a chocolate Slugshake
Kentucky-Fried Slug legs
Angel-Slug twinkies
Scrambled Slug eggs

Slick a Slug with Super Glue
Stick it on your sister Sue
Place another, maybe two
In her favorite high-heel shoe

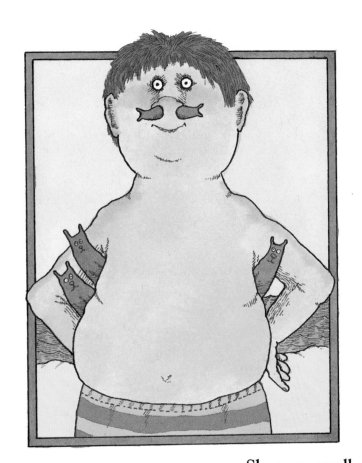

Slugs are small and portable
Just stuff 'em up your nose
They'll fit beneath your armpits
Or right between your toes

Fat Slugs
Skinny Slugs
Sad Slugs
Grinny Slugs

Dimpled ones
Crinkled ones
Gimpled ones
Wrinkled ones
Slugs are very beautiful
Even chubby pimpled ones

Sneeze a Slug
Slurp a Slug
Squeeze a Slug
Twirp a Slug
If you have a stomach-ache
You can even burp a Slug

17

Roast 'em
Toast 'em
Stew 'em
Chew 'em
Dump 'em in your mother's bath
Ask her to shampoo 'em

Suck your Slugs through straws
Mix them with spaghetti
Drop them off your balcony
Special Slug confetti!

19

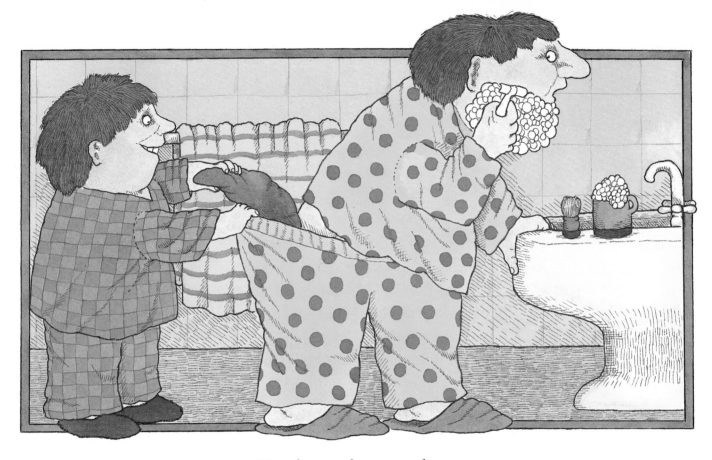

Use them in banana splits
Instead of ripe bananners
Or put one in your father's
Polka-dot pyjammers

Cover one with toothpaste
Or chocolate if it's handy
Then wrap it up in cellophane
"Won't you have some candy?"

Tie one to a bottle rocket
Launch it, Zappo Zingo!
Shoot one from a slingshot
Through a neighbor's window

Like to play Monopoly?
Then try the game with Slugs
You'll never have to move them
And they won't run off like bugs

23

They're excellent as bookmarks
For polishing antiques
They're comfortable as earplugs
And great for patching leaks

Some are square
Some have claws
Some are shaped like flutes
Some have hair
Some wear bras
Some wear three-piece suits

They live in houses, trailers, slums
Wealthy Slugs sail giant yachts
Slugs are cowboys, Slugs are bums
Slugs are even astronauts

Why, there are Slugs that know karate
There are Slugs as big as you
And some night when you're fast asleep
This is what they'll do:

They'll grab you by your chin
Butter you with germs
Throw you out the window
Mash you up with worms

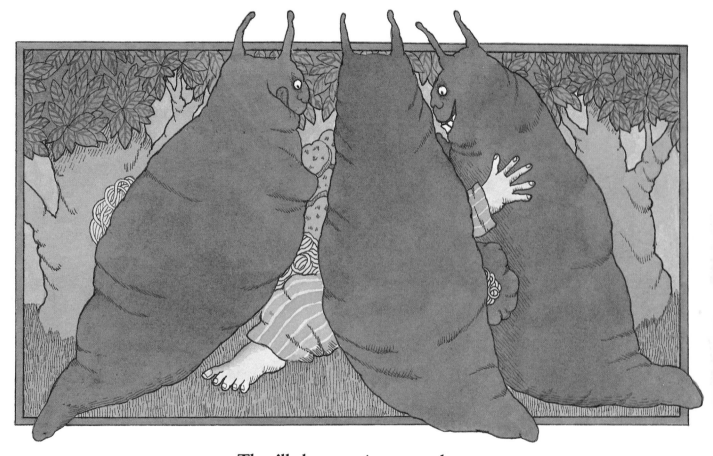

They'll chop you into pancakes
And turn you inside out
So your liver's on the outside
And your brain is sauerkraut

Then they'll put you back together
So your navel's in your nose
So your feet come out your ears
So your eyes are on your toes

Then they'll stuff you in a garbage can
And leave you overnight
And after how <u>you</u>'ve treated Slugs
It surely serves you right!

31